HIS DIRTY VIRGIN

THE VIRGIN PACT - BOOK 3

JESSA JAMES

GET A FREE BOOK!

Join my mailing list to be the first to know of new releases, free books, special prices and other author giveaways.

http://freehotcontemporary.com

His Dirty Virgin: Copyright © 2017 by Jessa James

ISBN: 978-1-7959-0197-0

All Rights Reserved. No part of this book may be reproduced or transmitted in any form or by any means, electrical, digital or mechanical including but not limited to photocopying, recording, scanning or by any type of data storage and retrieval system without express, written permission from the publisher.
Published by Orange Poodle LLC
James, Jessa
His Dirty Virgin

Cover design copyright 2017 by Jessa James, Author
Images/Photo Credit: CanstockPhoto.com-coka

Publisher's Note:

This book was written for an adult audience. The book may contain explicit sexual content. Sexual activities included in this book are strictly fantasies intended for adults and any activities or risks taken by fictional characters within the story are neither endorsed nor encouraged by the author or publisher.

This book has been previously published.

1

ecca

I FELT THE BLOWOUT MORE THAN HEARD IT. I EXPECTED a flat tire to have a huge boom or pop, but no. The wheel began to shake and my steering became erratic. Thankfully, I wasn't going too fast and the road was straight. I was able to pull off to the side without sliding into the ditch. I sat there, heart racing, adrenaline pumping, cars whizzing by.

I wanted to scream my lungs out. A flat! I didn't need this. I had more than enough on my plate already. I'd just come from lunch with my father, and as usual, it ended up with him telling me how much of a disappointment I was and me walking out of the restaurant. All I'd done was tell him I was taking up pre-med for my major, not that I decided not to go to college to be a carnie with the circus. No matter how uncomfortable the lunch, and his blatant disapproval, I still wasn't – and *never* would – go into business.

"Others would die to be in your position!" he'd told me at the restaurant. "While your classmates are scurrying to find an entry-level job or even an unpaid internship in the hopes they can land full-time offers four years from now when college is over, I'll put you in the fast track. You can be a manager next month. Why don't you want that?"

"I just graduated high school!" I'd responded, raising my voice. He'd been listening but hadn't heard me. He never had. "Can't I just have fun for a while?"

The expression on his face had morphed. The wrinkles on his forehead deepened, and every muscle on his body stiffened. The look wasn't new. I'd seen it countless times – sadness, disappointment, and hopelessness all mixed together – but it still always bothered me, as if I could never do right by him.

"Life isn't about 'having fun'. You'd know that if I didn't hand everything to you on a gold, diamond-encrusted platter. You never had to work a day in your life, Becca. Of course, all you want to do is 'have fun'. That's on me...to have given you everything. I feel like I've failed as a father."

Everything he'd given me came at a price and that

was going into the family business. If I joined him, he'd think it all had been worth it. If I didn't do it, then I was a slacker. A slacker who wanted to be a doctor, but still, to him, a freeloader. Spoiled. I couldn't have sat there a minute longer, so I walked out of the restaurant.

My dad had always put himself up on a pedestal. It was infuriating. But there was still that little voice in my head, that little voice telling me that I should listen to him, that he just loved me too much and wanted what was best for me. He loved me enough to want me to take over his empire someday. And that was why he'd given me everything I needed and wanted.

There was no denying he and my mom always gave me the best. They sent me to the best private school, they gave me all the gadgets and tools I'd needed and wanted to make studying easier, they hired the best coaches and personal trainers so that I'd become a state-level athlete. Even without my father paying my tuition, I'd had multiple academic and sports scholarships to choose from. Even after my mother died eight years ago and my father remarried, the help didn't stop. Anything I asked for, I got.

Yeah…maybe he failed as a father because he spoiled me too much, but I hadn't wasted any of it. I'd excelled at it all. I was going to be a damn doctor.

"Fuck." The profanity left my mouth when I

realized I'd been sitting in my car for too long, and I was starting to sweat.

It was June, the middle of the day with the summer sun was beating down, and here I was with a flat tire. I had a spare in the trunk, but I was definitely not in the mood to change it. I had no choice. Tires didn't change themselves.

I swung open the driver's door and shut it with a bang before I went to the trunk and unlocked it. With all the strength I could muster, I did my best to pull the tire out and rolled it as close as I could to the flat. I walked back to the trunk to look for the wrench. I could feel the sun burning my back, the sweat dripping down my face and arms. I wanted to be anywhere but here, do anything but this, except maybe go back to the restaurant with my dad. As I kept complaining in my head, I loosened up the nuts. They were on so tight, I wasn't sure if I could get them all.

"You need help?"

That voice. All male, deep and rumbly.

I dropped the tool with a clang and stood, tipped my head up, my eyes moving from muscled arms covered in tattoos to a sun-kissed angular jaw, and finally, striking pale blue eyes. I instantly stilled, my heart hammering once again. He was easily one of the most attractive men I'd ever seen, if not the most. And he had tattoos! They were a dangerous—but oh-so sexy—touch I never knew could be so hot.

"Y-yes, please," I managed to croak out.

He moved to glance down at the tire, then at me. "I'm Jake Huntington." He easily introduced himself, sticking his big hand out for me to shake. "Just so you can report my name to the police when I get in your car and drive off." My eyes instantly went wide, and he took notice. A wicked grin spread across his face. "Just kidding. I can't drive away with a flat tire." His eyes raked up and down my figure, from my mop of brown hair and all the way down to my wedge sandals.

"Seriously, it was a joke. Ever heard of one?"

I realized I was still staring, not responding. I shook my head. "I'm sorry, but this flat hasn't put me in a joking mood. This day's just getting worse, and it's barely after lunch."

"You and me both," he grumbled.

"I'm Becca, by the way. Becca Madison." I noticed the look on his face—recognition. It was the same expression I had just moments ago when he introduced himself.

Jake Huntington...the name definitely rang a bell. He looked like the same Jake I'd met back at my mother's funeral dinner years ago. The same eye and hair color. Only now, the teenager I once knew had grown into a man. Crazy for me to remember after so long, but he was...unforgettable. The Jake beside me now was *all* man. He was much taller, more muscular, and stood proud like he had his shit together. Maybe he did, even if he left home and turned his back on his family. Yeah, I'd heard the story because Jake's dad was my father's corporate attorney.

It had been big news in our small town—when Jake ran away. Well, he hadn't *run* away like a five-year-old. He'd been studying pre-law when he decided he didn't want to become a lawyer and his father had flipped. I didn't know the details of what happened after that, but I hadn't heard a peep about Jake since. All I knew was that he wasn't considered part of the family anymore.

"Whatever happened to law school?"

A slow smile spread across his face. "I'm infamous enough that a pretty girl on the side of the road knows who I am."

I shrugged. "You know who I am by my name, just as I know you."

He slowly shook his head. "You don't know me. Just what you've heard."

I looked him over from his boots to his very well-worn jeans to his black t-shirt which left nothing to the imagination. "You're right. So what happened to law school?"

A smirk made its way onto his face at my repeated question. *Damn*, he was hot. "Nothing. I decided not to go and instead started my own business after I got my degree."

"Oh? What business?" I guessed his life was turning

out much better than mine ever would. I didn't think I could do what he did, turn my back on my family and make it on my own. Telling my father off at lunch was one thing, but go solo? I had no idea how I'd make it. Maybe my father was right. He'd given me everything, and I didn't know how to stand on my own two feet.

He stuck his elbow out. "Does my arm say enough?" I couldn't miss the corded forearms, the bulging biceps. *A gym?* "Tattoo parlor."

I nodded my head. "Was it your mother that steered you in that direction?"

He looked shocked at my question until a smile surfaced once again on his face. "You remember my mother?"

"Of course." I smiled back. "I might be younger than you, but our families are pretty close. Your mom, she's...definitely a character."

His mother was the antithesis of what our fathers were like. They were masters of the universe. At least of this town. They were powerful and rich. They were the type of people that no one could say no to, even if their demands seemed unrealistic. People under them just had to make things happen.

"Definitely." At that, we both shared a laugh. "But yeah, she nurtured my interest in the arts, taught me how to enjoy life and not take it so seriously. Because of that, I started drawing when I needed to de-stress. She'd bring me along when she went out with some friends sometimes. I knew I'd get bored sooner or later, so I'd always bring my sketchpad, and when they saw my art, all of them were asking me if I could tattoo my artwork."

"Oh, wow…so your business started organically."

We stood on the side of the road chatting until he suddenly remembered the tire. He grabbed the tire iron and knelt by the flat, got to work.

He seemed like a nice guy and he'd gotten out from under his father's wrath. I envied him that.

"Yeah, they'd see my art, but there was always a deeper meaning whenever they chose their designs, and that—the stories and meanings behind the tattoos—turned my hobby into a passion. People sharing their experiences through art is such a great way to connect. It's as if once they see you have a tattoo, their walls instantly come down. Even if they're doing it as a dare or out of drunkenness, they're still showing some kind of vulnerability—they're giving me and everyone else the opportunity to judge, and that's the thing—I never judge. I embrace." I was too engrossed listening to him I hadn't realized he was finished with replacing my tire. "There you go, princess."

I raised my eyebrow up at him. *Princess?* I followed his eyes and watched as they lingered for a moment on the pearls on my ears and around my neck and then my pale pink sundress. *Oh.*

"Stop by sometime." He reached in his back pocket

and took a card out from his wallet. "The shop. I saw the look on your face earlier. You're curious. Come check it out for yourself."

"Sure," I responded, meeting his eyes. I mustered up the courage to smile at him. *God*. I could stare at him all day. I was curious. Not as much about a tattoo as about him, and exactly what it would feel like to have a certified bad boy kissed me. "I will. I'll stop by."

2

ecca

EVERY TIME I THOUGHT ABOUT JAKE, MY BRAIN WAS telling me 'no', but my pussy was giving me a big 'yes'!

I'd been lying in bed for a good couple of hours, not wanting to get up. The morning was half gone already, but I didn't care. I hadn't slept much the night before, but I wasn't tired. I was kidding myself thinking my frustration was with my father and the conversation at lunch was keeping me awake, but it wasn't that. It wasn't my demanding, judgmental, arrogant father. Not at all. I'd been living with his stern stares and long lectures for years. No, my mind kept picturing a certain blond-haired, blue-eyed man I barely knew.

Just thinking about Jake made me wet. He'd looked so good when he stopped to help me change my tire. Beads of sweat had run down his golden skin as we stood under the scorching midday sun. His hands had been covered in oil and grease from fixing my tire, but it did nothing to mar his looks. The truth was the dirt and grime made him look dangerously sexier. He'd been willing to get down and dirty for me like a bad boy gentleman.

But he was older. Not like a creepy father figure or something, but he was twenty-four. At least. It was as if the age difference made him off-limits, forbidden fruit. No, it was more that I was too young, a virgin just out of high school. And he'd called me a princess.

To him, I probably was. But that didn't mean I felt like one.

He was so different from the guys in the all-boys school we usually had dances with. They always looked so kept, with not a single strand of hair on their heads out of place. The polos and blazers they wore never creased. I couldn't help but imagine a few of my guy friends trying to change my tire, and I burst out laughing. I just couldn't fathom them getting down and dirty. I doubted they even knew how to do it. They'd probably have their chauffeurs change my tire instead.

But Jake...

I shook my head as his name made me sigh.

Nothing about the way he changed my tire was humorous. He'd been oh-so sexy, efficient, and so...*manly*. I laughed imagining him putting the boys in the private school to shame. He'd been one himself, graduating and then going his own way. Giving his father and the country club lifestyle the finger.

The bad boy image worked for him. Every part of him seemed to have been carved by a master sculptor, and what made it even better was that all his tattoos seemed to fit perfectly with his physique. Yes. Him. *Definitely.*

I should have been interested in the boys who I graduated with. Off to Harvard or Princeton and then back to work in the family law firm, just as Jake had been expected to do. I was expected to work at my father's firm until I married, after which, I'd never use my college education for more than popping out two children and taking them to the country club pool.

No, I didn't want that any more than Jake did. He'd walked away. I wanted to. I didn't want any of the guys my father pushed my way. I felt no attraction. No desire. Nothing. I wanted someone who made my breath catch, my heart race, my nipples harden and my pussy ache. If I was going to fulfill the stupid virgin pact I'd made with a few of my girlfriends before graduation, it was going to be difficult with the Todds and Chads I knew. So far, there hadn't been anyone worthy. I wasn't going to hand my V-card over to just any guy.

My friends Jane and Mary had already done it. Snagged the right guys and given it up. From the way they looked at their men—and they *were* men—they'd enjoyed it immensely. Jane had been the first, snagging our Civics and Government teacher, Mr. Parker. Mary, on the other hand, had been set up with Greg, Mr. Parker's friend. Well, it wasn't really a setup. Mary was babysitting Greg's niece, and things had progressed rapidly from there.

Now, both were madly in love with their respective boyfriends, and they wanted me to find the same. They were always gushing about going on dates together, and that dating older men came with certain perks... both outside and inside the bedroom. From eating in classy, expensive restaurants to experimenting with hot sex, they boasted how it was better with older men. I believed them. No one could ever go wrong with experience, but the competitive part of me wanted the extra challenge of finding my own...*virgin taker*?

I laughed at the thought. Virgin-taker sounded so... medieval, but that basically summed up what I was looking for. He didn't have to be older like Mr. Parker or Greg. He just had to be the right guy. My thoughts immediately went to Jake. Yeah, I finally found the guy who I wanted to give my virginity to.

I'd have no issues having my first time with Jake. I remembered how effortlessly he replaced my tire. He was strong and *very* good with his hands. He'd probably be able to carry and throw me onto his bed with one hand. I had no doubt he knew exactly what to do. A guy that gorgeous couldn't have been single all these years. I hoped he knew his way around a woman's body because that would make for an excellent first time.

What was even better was what my father would think of me hooking up with the black sheep, tattoo covered rebel like Jake.

Since our fathers worked closely together, mine never failed to talk about that "rebel kid." He never said Jake's name. He always ranted about how ungrateful Jake was to turn his back on his family. His parents, just like mine, had paid for everything. They'd put him in the best schools, groomed him for success he'd have no problem achieving. My father had even been ready to give him a position in his company as one of the heads of the legal department.

"He just walked away from everything, from an easy life of power, wealth, and success…to what?" My father had said on numerous occasions. Back then, his words never really bothered me because I only remembered Jake as another face from the funeral, nothing more. But now, they stung because I was in a similar position.

I wanted to carve out my own path, one very different from what my father had been preparing for me my whole life. If he'd been so harsh with Jake, I wondered how he'd be with me, his own daughter. I had a feeling our lunch argument was only the beginning.

I forced myself to get up. I'd holed myself up in my room too long already that the thoughts in my head were making me grumpier. I needed to get out, and immediately I knew where to go. Who I needed to see. Hell, I'd spent all morning thinking about him.

An hour later, I found myself standing in front of his tattoo parlor, R.

R—the name of his business. It was catchy, yet its simplicity put the spotlight on where it was rightfully supposed to be—the artwork. I gathered enough courage to suck it up and go inside. What if he didn't want to see me? What if he thought of me as a little kid? Or worse, a princess? I thought of calling and making an appointment to get a tattoo, and I didn't even know if I wanted one. Now that I was here, being inspired by the artwork on display, I was certain I wanted some ink, and I knew specifically the design I wanted.

"Hey, good morning! Do you have an appointment?" the lady at the reception asked. She wore a white tank top that showed off the tattoos on her left arm and down over the back of her hand. "I'm Anna, by the way."

"Becca," I shared as I looked around the big room. "I'm just a drop in, if that's okay?"

Honestly, the space was far from what I expected, and a little part of me felt ashamed at my own judgmental self. The place was sleek, modern, and upscale. The walls were in a dark gray palette with the ceiling in stark white. Ambient yellow lighting set the mood with white-light lamps strategically positioned right above the chairs and tables where people got tattooed. It was clean, neat. My eyes roamed the entire place, and they finally found *him*.

Jake was busy talking to a client as he smeared some ointment on a fresh tattoo, then wrapped it in plastic wrap. I thought of going over to him, but I didn't want to interrupt.

"Sure, drop ins are fine. Have you met any of the artists before?" With that, I turned my head to look at Anna. "Most of the customers want last-minute appointments after randomly meeting one of our artists, so the schedule's quite packed. It's great though…very effective marketing." The two of us shared a smile at that before I nodded my head.

"Worked for me," I agreed. "I have a design in mind, but I can't draw to save my life. Do you think I can speak to one of the artists and have him draw what I want?"

Anna beamed. "Absolutely. Want to see our artists'

portfolios? They're all amazing, so your choice depends on the style and aesthetic you want."

I didn't need to look to know what I wanted. *Who* I wanted. "Jake...Jake Huntington," came my instant response. "I want him."

"Hmm...Jake..." she trailed off, moving her head to look at her desktop computer. "Unfortunately, he's fully booked for the rest of the week. He's available next Thursday. Is that alright? You'll have time to iron out the details of the design you want."

I couldn't help but feel disappointed. I'd made up my mind and waiting a week would only give me the time I needed to chicken out. Not about the tattoo, but about the rest. In this moment, I was bold, but would it last? Would I be able to come back and tell him I wanted him for more than just a tattoo? "He's pretty busy, huh?"

"Yeah. It's great, actually. He's very hands on even if he's the owner."

Hands on. Good. I wanted him to be *very* hands on.

"He could let the other artists do his work for him, but he enjoys what he does. 'Enjoy' is even an understatement."

Becca couldn't help but smile at that. *Can the guy get any more attractive?* His looks were more than enough, and now, his passion for what he does? *Damn*, was all I could think.

If I couldn't have Jake in bed, then I could still get a tattoo.

"Who's free to tattoo me tonight? I don't think I want to wait," I said, smiling sheepishly.

I felt the back of my neck burn, and when I turned around, Jake was looking right at me. I sucked in a harsh breath at his steel gaze. He started walking towards me.

3

ake

Becca was here. Not in a prim sundress, but a pair of denim shorts that barely covered her ass and a silky baby blue tank top. Holy shit.

"Bob!" Anna shouted out from behind the reception desk. "Come over here! Someone wants some ink!"

Fuck. My eyes moved from Becca to Bob a few times before they settled on the six-footer walking over to Anna and Becca a little too eagerly. He said a few words to Anna before he turned to the familiar brunette. Her wavy hair was brushed to her left shoulder; her cute, pointy chin added just the right amount of sexiness to her innocent brown eyes. I didn't miss the way Bob's eyes moved to glance at her tits for a second. He could probably feel the hole I was burning in his skull since he tipped his head up and his eyes landed on mine.

Fuck off. My gaze said enough. That silenced him, and he began scratching the back of his head as I walked over to them.

"Fancy seeing you here," I said with just a ghost of a smirk tainting my lips. *Fuck, I could just waste my whole day staring at her.* She wasn't beautiful in the usual sense, but fuck, my dick liked her just fine. And every caveman instinct that lay dormant roared to life. I didn't even want Bob looking at her, let alone marking her skin with ink. "Sure you're in the right place, princess?"

"Shut up, boss," Anna was quick to say. "She wants a tattoo by you specifically, but you're fully booked this whole week."

I saw her flush, glance away, but after a moment, she lifted her chin and met my gaze.

"You told me to stop by," Becca quickly put in, and my smirk instantly widened. *Never thought she'd be the kind to stand up for herself.*

She dressed and acted...well, fuck, she definitely fit the helpless persona to a tee, and she looked exactly that yesterday. When I saw her on the side of the road in her pearls and pink dress and trying her goddamn best to change her tire, my decision had been a no-brainer. She was a pretty girl who'd needed help.

Then I discovered that the *she* I'd helped was none other than Becca Madison. I hadn't seen her in years and in that time, she'd changed. A whole hell of a lot. She wasn't a little girl anymore. She had legs as long as sin and curves in all the right places.

I wanted her to be the helpless one, to seek me out when she had a problem. Yeah, I was full of shit because it was just random luck that I'd come upon her the day before. But I didn't want anyone helping her. I wanted her to turn to me, to *need* me. Only me.

But she *was* a fucking princess. Her damn car cost *more* than a hundred G's. I'd owned and driven luxury vehicles when I lived with my parents and they'd been supporting me, and I had to admit I kind of missed that need for speed. My pickup truck was practical, but I wasn't going to be breaking any fucking land-speed records anytime soon with it.

That wasn't worth the price tag that came with it. And I wasn't talking about money. It was being under my father's thumb. I'd walked away and I wasn't going back. Not even for a killer car.

I shook my head to cut my train of thought. How the hell was I thinking about a car when I had a beautiful woman standing in front of me? Everyone was staring at me expectantly and I felt like an idiot. This girl got my mind wandering.

Then I focused in on what Anna had said. Becca came in to get a tattoo. I felt my heart skip a beat. I was the one she wanted touching her skin, marking her. But I didn't want to dirty her. My hands were calloused from all the hard labor I enjoyed doing, be it working on my car, exercising in my home gym a floor above the studio, and tattooing. I felt like the moment I touched her that her innocence and sweetness would instantly vanish.

But if I didn't do it, Bob would be all over helping her out. And that shit wasn't going to fly.

"Come on into the back room. I'll do your ink there." I wanted to be alone with her. I wasn't sure where she wanted her tattoo, but no one was getting a glimpse of any more of her skin. Besides, I didn't want anyone else to see my hard-on. As soon as I touched her, I'd be in big trouble.

She walked beside me and I let her enter the room first. It was used for when a client wanted a little privacy—a tattoo going in a more personal spot or even a piercing.

"I'm going to grab my sketch pad so we can talk design. I'll be right back."

When I left the room, I could see Anna and Bob looking at me suspiciously. I responded with a smirk before I hurried over to my office and grabbed my stuff. I was back with her in no time, and she looked like she was making herself comfortable in the chair.

"Do you know what you want?"

She nodded her head and began to unbutton her shorts and pulled her zipper down. "I want a butterfly on my hip...for my mother. She used to call me 'my little butterfly'."

She wriggled herself to move her shorts below her hips and let them stay there.

Fuuuuck. I swore her bright pink panties were going to be the death of me. Her shorts were tight and lifted her ass cheeks up a bit. *What...the...*

"I want it right here." The tip of her pointer finger rested lightly on her hip bone. "Will it hurt?"

I just stared and stared at the exposed flesh. The curve of her hip was something I could easily grab hold of when fucking her from behind. The thong covered her mound and made me wonder if it was wet, ruined with her eagerness for me to fuck her. She certainly wasn't overly modest. Thank fuck I brought her to the back room. Shit, if Bob got sight of her with her shorts down, I'd have punched him out.

I cleared my throat, gently ran my finger over the spot where she wanted the ink. Silky soft. Warm. I was going to come like a fucking teenager if I didn't pull it together. "I remember your mother...she was... definitely much nicer than your father." We exchanged grins at that. "So, regretting coming in tonight?"

She was quick to shake her head, just watched my finger as it moved. "Nah. I just want to know exactly what I'm signing up for. Some of my friends say getting a tattoo hurts like a bitch, but others were able to take a nap while getting one."

"Well, it depends…" I placed my sketch pad on the desk and walked closer to her. I pressed two fingers on the skin of her hip bone once again, and fuck was I doing my best *not* to move my hand lower, to feel the lips of her pussy through the lace of her thong, to feel the wetness.

What the fuck did she really come here for?

I tried my best to keep my groan at bay and pressed my lower torso against the chair. My hard dick was relentless, and Becca wasn't helping. *She* was the cause of it.

"It depends where you want it. If it's near any bones, then yeah, it's more painful, but you'll live, and you can tell me to stop anytime. You can come more than once."

Fuck. The thought of her coming on my cock, on my mouth had me stifling a groan. And her coming more than once? Absolutely. When I got her in my bed, she was going to forget her own name.

I could see her hesitation with the way she bit her bottom lip. I coughed out loud to shadow another groan threatening to escape. She looked so beautiful and adorable that I just wanted to push her back against the chair and climb on top of her, to slide those shorts down a little further and slip right into her tight heat.

Fuck off, inner me said, and I was instantly reminded that girls like her never went for guys like me. I wasn't rich and dangerous for someone like her. I had no future ahead of me besides my small business. No trips to Europe, no polo ponies. There was no way she could go to her high-society events and bring me as her date. I'd just humiliate her. She couldn't be with the guy who'd walked away from it all.

Cut it out. She just wants a tattoo, not a relationship.

That thought was supposed to be an instant boner killer, but with her shorts pulled down that was impossible.

"Are you sure you want to do this? You look nervous," I said, realizing my fingers were still on her hip bone. I didn't want to pull them away. "Give yourself a week to think it over and give me a call. I'll work around your availability."

Suddenly, the shy, helpless girl before me disappeared. There was a light in her eyes and a steadfastness with the way she looked at me now, the way she shifted her hips into my touch.

"I want you," she said.

Um... There was no way I could look away. What the fuck was she talking about?

"My friends and I made a pact." Her pink tongue

darted out to lick her lips. "To lose our virginity before college starts. I want it to be you. The one to fuck me first."

What. The. Fuck? "Say that again, princess."

"I want you to be the one who fucks me first."

4

Becca

I COULDN'T TAKE MY EYES OFF JAKE, ESPECIALLY NOT after what I'd just said. It was the truth. I really wanted to get a tattoo, a butterfly, but having him fuck me ranked higher in my list of priorities. I told him what I wanted and it was up to him if he'd give it to me.

Waiting for him to respond felt like an eternity, as if everything was in slow motion. I watched as he swallowed, his Adam's apple bobbing once. I imitated him, then sucked in a breath of my own. I'd been bold, bolder than I'd ever been in my life, but I'd learned from my father I had to go after what I wanted. I doubted he meant going after a guy to fuck me, but...

whatever. My gaze drifted lower, moved down from his neck past his broad shoulders, muscled torso, narrow waist to the growing bulge in his jeans. Wow. My heart beat faster at the sight.

I'd gotten to him. I made him horny if the size of his dick was any indication.

I reached out, carefully and a little hesitantly, and wrapped my fingers around his wrist. He could stop me at any time—he was so much stronger than me—but he didn't. I moved his hand down, the pads of his skin just barely touching my hip bone, and further south until he hovered over my pussy, then pressed down. *There.* I closed my eyes at the sensation. I'd never had a guy touch me like this before. It was featherlight, but my pussy felt like they were on fire. I smiled a bit when I heard a groan escape his lips.

His eyes met mine, but he remained still, let me move his hand as I wanted over my shorts. He could tug his hand free, I wouldn't be able to stop him. He could control me easily, but in this moment, but he was letting me take the lead. What guy wouldn't if it led to pussy?

Bold, I pulled my shorts all the way down to reveal lacy see-through thong. "I went shopping today," I murmured, glancing up and watching his eyes, the way they heated, his jaw, the way it clenched as he looked at me. Saw what no other man had seen before.

I'd gotten a Brazilian yesterday after he changed my

tire and with the way his eyes and his big bulge grew even bigger, I knew I made the right decision to go bare.

"Touch me…" I didn't move his hand. Starting now, whatever happened next was up to him. "Please."

He stared at me with the same intensity I gave him, and with every second of silence passing, I grew wetter and hotter. His striking blue eyes raked over me as if he were memorizing every inch. A part of me wanted to know what he was thinking, but with the way he was making me feel, I wanted to leave the talking for later… after…we'd done what I wanted him to do.

"You're a virgin," he said, voice trailing off as if he was talking more to himself than to me. His fingers remained still, but I could feel the heat of them through the thin fabric barrier.

I nodded my head. "Yes."

"Have you done other things?" I unwound my fingers from his wrist, but his hand still stayed on my pussy. "Been finger fucked?"

I shook my head.

"Given a blow job?"

I shook my head again.

"Had your pussy eaten?"

Once more.

"What *have* you done?"

His gaze flicked up to mine.

I bit my lip, slightly embarrassed. I was eighteen

and a virgin. A very virgin *virgin*. He was older, experienced, worldly. Hell, he probably had women flinging themselves at him all day long. I'd done it just now, but I was just a clueless. Was I doing it right? Why would he want me? I fit the "loser" stereotype perfectly. I suddenly felt like cowering away, hunching my shoulders into a defensive position. This was silly. *I* was silly even asking him to do this. To expose myself to him like this. I tried to get up, but he moved quickly, his free hand grasping my shoulder to keep me still. He hovered over me. I was trapped, his broad chest much wider than mine, and his arms were big and strong to keep me in place. I felt like I couldn't escape him, and I liked the feeling. I'd been bold to begin with, but it seemed he was taking over.

"You've never been touched before?" he asked, even though he already knew the answer. "Here?" His fingers pressed against my pussy, and I was trying my best not to squirm. "Or here?" The hand on my shoulder slid lower to cup my right breast.

I shook my head again, bit my lip again. I didn't cower anymore, but arched my back so I filled his palm more fully.

"Will you?" I whispered.

He looked from my pussy and up into my eyes.

"Will you touch me?"

The edges of his lips curved upward into a grin. "Fuck yes," came his response. "This?" He brushed over my clit. "This pussy's all mine." With that, his fingers slipped underneath the edge of my thong and really touched me. It was a heated shock, just that light touch.

"You're drenched for me, baby."

I pushed my head backward, closed my eyes. I wanted to remember this moment, every bit of what it felt like to be pleasured. By a man. Not by my hand any longer. I jumped a bit in the chair when his two fingers lightly pinched my clit.

"Relax," he breathed, before holding me against the chair. "Don't feel nervous. You're safe with me. Enjoy everything I'm about to give you."

I glanced down, saw his tattooed arm and followed it down to see his hand between my legs, his fingers disappearing beneath the pink lace. It was so hot, being touched by the bad boy, I whimpered.

"Shh. Your pleasure belongs to me. Only me. I don't want anyone else to hear it."

Not wasting a second, he pushed my top above my breasts and expertly unhooked the front clasp of my bra. I opened my eyes and watched as his head lowered to hover near just over my taut nipple. His eyes met mine for just a second before he parted his lips and took the tip into his mouth.

"Fu-…yes…Ry—an…" It was getting harder and harder for me to form anything coherent—and to remain quiet. I couldn't speak properly. *Hell*. I didn't want to. Jake told me to relax and just enjoy, and I was going to do exactly that. I closed my eyes tighter as I relished the feel of my nipples getting sucked and my pussy being touched at the same time. I inhaled sharply and then elicited a soft moan when he slipped a finger inside me and started to move it in and out, mimicking what I wanted him to do with his cock. I arched my back off the chair, trying to push his finger deeper inside me with a thrust of my hips. I heard him let out a short laugh, and I wasn't prepared when he slipped another finger in.

"You're so tight. Virgin tight."

"Oh...Go—" I breathed, louder this time, when he started to move his hand faster and faster. I couldn't help but open my eyes, and I watched him continue to suck on my nipple. He pulled his mouth away from my chest and looked up at me.

"You're so fucking wet...getting a little noisy, too," he said, smile widening all the more. "Just imagine when I get my dick inside you. This tight little cunt is going to be split in two, babe. I'm big and this pussy, I'm going to take that cherry. Don't worry, I'll fit...eventually."

"Yes...yes, please..." I thrust my hips riding the pleasure. His dirty talk only pushed me close to the brink. "I don't want to be a virgin anymore."

"Greedy, aren't you?" He let out a 'tsk' and shook his head. "You need my big dick, don't you? You'll just have to be patient," he said, continuing to finger me, as he flicked my clit with his thumb. "I'm not fucking you for the first time in the back room of a tattoo shop. I want to give you the best first time ever...and when I do, it's going to last all night."

He looked down my body and focused on my pussy, watched his fingers sink inside me over and over. With his thumb exerting pressure on my clit, I was about to come. But this was so much better than any orgasm I ever gave myself.

Is this...? Am I...?

I couldn't control my moans any longer, not the frequency or the volume. He took it as his cue to move faster and delve deeper inside me until I had to grip his biceps to keep from flying away.

"Oh God...Jake...I'm gonna co—"

I broke then, riding his fingers, giving over to the pleasure. I had no idea it would be like this, that there were places deep inside me that made it incredible. I could barely catch my breath as his fingers began to slow down their movements. After a while, I found the energy to open my eyes. They zoned in on his hand, slicked with my juices, and watched as he lifted it to his mouth, sucked each finger clean.

"I almost came in my pants by listening to you," he said, chuckling a bit.

"Well, we can't let that happen yet," I said, a little coy. "I want to do that again, but this time with your cock in me. You told me—"

"Didn't I say to just relax?" he said in a teasing manner. He grinned as he adjusted himself, the steel beam that was practically ripping out of his jeans. *That* was going to fit? "Later. When I can get you in my bed and you won't have to leave."

I nodded my head, smiled. My pussy clenched eagerly for what was to come. "But I still want the tattoo, really."

He let out an amused bark. "Of course, but I don't think that's your priority at the moment. Is it? You're pussy's still needy?"

I bit my lip, nodded. What he'd just done only made me eager for more.

He helped me up, gave me a swat on the ass. "Later. Definitely later."

5

I DIDN'T KNOW WHAT WAS GETTING MORE DAMAGE, MY fucking knuckles or the punching bag. I'd been going at it relentlessly for the past fifteen minutes. Sooner rather than later, I was going to bleed.

What the fuck had I been thinking?

A few hours ago, there was no way I could ever, *ever* touch Becca...and for her own good. She was unbreakable china, immaculate and fragile, and I was the bad boy. I was everything that wasn't good for her. My family disowned me. I wasn't mingling with the higher-ups of society. I had tattoos. I was nothing but dangerous for her. And I'd dirtied her. I got her nice and filthy.

And she'd loved it.

I saw the look on her face when she came for a man for the first time. She'd done it because of me. For me. Her eyes had been closed but her mouth remained open, moans of pleasure escaping those plump lips. I should have covered her mouth or kissed her or something because there was no way everyone in the tattoo parlor hadn't heard her. It was arrogant of me, but a moaning woman was always a badge of honor.

But she wasn't just a fling and I sure as fuck didn't want to share her.

There was just something about Becca. She was like a drug. Just the feel of her virgin pussy creaming all over my fingers and I was hooked. Yet, I couldn't have her. She was a fucking princess. She had her life mapped out for her. With the support and money of her family, she was certain of a bright, successful future. She was gorgeous, smart, and wealthy – the perfect triple threat. I was completely no good for her.

But she told me outright she wanted me. She'd come to me. She'd come all over my hand.

She wanted me for sex. If she wanted to troll and use me to see what a big dick felt like before she settled down to vanilla sex the rest of her life, that was fine. But I was irrationally possessive, it seemed. I knew, once I slipped into that tight pussy, got that sweet honey coat my dick and broke through that cherry of hers, she was all mine.

Fuck this. Why couldn't I stop thinking about her? I gave up my workout and headed for the shower.

Becca was just a girl, a virgin…a virgin girl who'd told me straight up she wanted me to fuck her. How could someone be so innocent and sexy at the same time? The fucking kicker was, she had no ideal her appeal, her charm. Her passion. A passion that I'd awakened.

I shook my head and closed my eyes tight. *This* wasn't helping. I had to stop daydreaming about her. She was taking up all my thoughts and that needed to stop. *Wake up.* I wasn't a horny teenager anymore. I was twenty-four years old with tattoos all over me. It made me 'dangerously sexy' or so I'd been told. I could have sex with more experienced women. Hell, I just had to pull out my cell for any number of women on speed dial who'd drop to their knees and suck me down. I needed to stop thinking about Becca…and her wavy brown hair and cute pointed chin and her innocent hazel eyes. Her pink nipples and the way they'd hardened against my tongue, her barely-legal pussy and how it had all but broken my fingers when she came. The flavor of her as I licked her juices from my fingers. The scent of her that still lingered.

Fuck. *Fuck. STOP!*

I knew what I needed to do.

I'd think about her for a few more minutes, then stop completely. Turning on the shower, I waited for it to get scorching hot, then I stepped beneath the spray.

A groan escaped me when my fingers gripped my dick and started to move up and down. I shut my eyes tight, remembering what happened. After this...after I busted a nut, I could stop fantasizing about her and her sweet, wet pussy.

Fuck. I felt myself grow even harder, as I remembered how she'd spread her legs wide as I fingered her. She was tight, and if my dick got in there... I couldn't help but smirk. I couldn't wait till then. She'd already been wet with just the fingering. I wanted to feel her clench and milk my dick of my cum, to drain my balls dry. I wanted to hear her moan and to watch her close her eyes tight in pleasure. I wanted her to scream my name, only my name. I wanted her to dig her nails in my back, marking me as I would mark her deep inside that broken-in pussy.

"Fuck...yes..." I groaned, tightening my grip on my cock and moving my hand much faster now. "Becca...fuck...yes..."

I pictured me thrusting persistently in and out of her. She was lying on the chair in my tattoo parlor again, but this time, I was completely hovering above her and her legs were wrapped around my waist. Her fingers were right on my ass pulling me closer to her, as if I could go any deeper.

Another beast-like growl escaped as I felt myself about to finish. *Thrust harder. Thrust faster.* I banged my palm on the glass of the shower as I came, the creamy liquid mixing with the hot, steaming water.

Fuck. It wasn't going to stop. My cock was still hard and I knew it would stay that way until I had her. After I came, I was supposed to stop fantasizing about an eighteen-year old virgin. I was supposed to stop thinking about wanting to fuck a spoiled, rich princess I could never keep. I was supposed to realize how wrong the situation was. But I couldn't avoid her. I'd have her. My dick wanted what my dick wanted.

She wants you, too. She told you she wants you to take her virginity. I could have her. She told me so. That was fine and all, but I wanted to keep her. I didn't want anyone else having her, not even so much as touch her. I wanted her to be all mine…and I was too much of an asshole to let her go. But I would ensure she'd love every inch of my dick as it crammed her full.

BECCA.

STOP SECOND GUESSING YOURSELF.

After I left the tattoo parlor, I spent the remaining hours shopping. I couldn't stop thinking about how into it Jake had been, fingering me with expert precision until I came. Then—then!—he'd said he wanted to stretch out my first time. Most guys would have climbed on top and just fucked me in the chair.

God, he looked like I'd hit him with a two-by-four when I told him I was a virgin and I was untouched. It was like I was a unicorn, a rare find. My girlfriends and I had made the pact to lose our virginities because there was a stigma surrounding virgins in college. The movies and the media said enough, but it seemed like Jake preferred the opposite, that I was a virgin.

But if I was going to give it to him, then I needed to blow his socks off. Or at least his load, deep inside me. God, that one orgasm had made me horny. I went shopping for a white sundress and matching sandals. The outfit, with not a single mark or crease, was enough to symbolize purity. And I was that…*right*? Pure, except for the fingering in the back room of a tattoo parlor. I wanted to be innocent on the outside, to everyone who saw me, but naughty for Jake with my matching hot, red lingerie that only he would see. The set was in lace, and I read somewhere that red was the color to turn men on.

But now, sitting across from Jake, I tried not to frown. I didn't want him to think I wasn't enjoying the dinner– steak and vegetables. I loved it. He'd gone the extra mile and cooked for me. I was just disappointed since I might have overdone the innocent look. We'd been eating and talking for over an hour, and not once had he mentioned what happened back in the tattoo parlor or even to talk about what I'd come here to do. He hadn't swiped the plates and cutlery to the floor and made a meal out of me. He'd done nothing but be a gentleman.

"Becca, you alright?"

Shit. I'd been too deep in my own thoughts.

"Hey, sorry..." I responded, moving my eyes away from my plate to meet his azure-colored ones. "I was side-tracked for a moment. This steak is delicious."

If there was one thing attending high-end events with my father had taught me, it was how to steer and carry conversation. I didn't want Jake to think I hadn't been listening to him because the truth was he was all I could think about.

"Good. I can make it again next time, or do you think I should switch it up from time to time?"

My eyes widened.

Did he mean...?

"I'm not taking that sweet cherry and running, doll baby," he then said, and I instantly felt my pussy squeeze in anticipation. I suddenly remembered what happened just hours ago, the way he fingered me and played with my clit. He hadn't even eaten me out or had sex with me yet, and he was already able to make me come. I could just imagine and dream about what having sex with him would feel like...for now.

. . .

In no time, I wouldn't just daydream about it, I'd *be having* sex with him. "I want to have sex with you every time and any time I want."

With every word he spoke, I was growing hotter and wetter. It was like music to my ears, what he was telling me. I had no plans for the summer. I just wanted to prepare for college and change my father's mind of forcing me into business. I was ready for a boring summer while some of my batchmates were going on crazy, international trips to mark the end of high school. I was ready to indulge myself with my endless list of tv shows, shopping, and trying to find a guy in this town to have sex with me.

And I was getting much more than I ever expected and wanted.

"What…do you mean?" I said slowly. The look in his eyes told me there was something more to his words.

"Move in with me…for one month."

I stayed silent, working the logistics in my head. I knew my father had multiple business trips lined up. He'd be out of town or out of the country more days than he'd be home. I could definitely do it – stay with Jake – and for the days my father was home, I could just tell him I was sleeping over at Jane's or Mary's or another friend's place.

So, I nodded my head. He looked shocked I agreed so quickly.

"That means sex any time…whenever I want and wherever."

My brain told me warning bells were supposed to start going off at this point, but my pussy only squeezed tighter. I was so turned on by his demands and how possessive he looked and spoke. I always thought men in their twenties were out of my league since they were more mature and wouldn't want anything from a clueless virgin. Looking at Jake now, I was starting to realize how wrong I was. His animal instinct for wanting me all for himself was making me feel better and was pushing my insecurities to the side. Even the way he looked before in his tattoo parlor when I told him no one else had ever touched me… there was a fire in his eyes, as if he wasn't ever going to let anyone do what he just did and was going to do with me.

"And we're not going to use condoms. I want my dick to feel your pussy just as my fingers did a while ago. You have to be on birth control."

My grin grew wider. I'd been on the pill for a couple years to control my periods. I was ready. I couldn't wait any longer.

"Done."

6

I WAS A BALL OF NERVES ON THE INSIDE. THIS WAS IT. It was finally going to happen. I was going to have sex. And my first time was going to be with *him*.

In one quick swoop, I was in Jake's arms as he carried me over to his bed. As my hands tightly grasped his shoulders, my insides felt like they were about to explode in excitement. His broad chest and shoulders were tight and muscular, and so was the rest of his entire body. I just couldn't believe that I was going to have sex with *him*. I couldn't have found and picked a better guy. He seemed impossible to reach. He put off such a dangerous and tough aura that I felt so stupid and inexperienced compared to him. I was eight years younger and a virgin. He had the looks and body of a model and the experience girls would lust over. He was the type of guy that if you saw him walking down the street, you'd just start thinking dirty thoughts immediately.

And I was going to get down and dirty *with* him.

I couldn't help the smile that came onto my face. He probably sensed it as he turned his head to look at me.

"Excited?"

Right before I was about to answer, he dropped me on the bed, and I couldn't help but squeal. "Jake!"

A laugh escaped his lips as he crawled on top of me and started exploring my body with his eyes and hands. My breathing turned heavier as I felt his hand explore my neck, down the curve of my waist, and then the inside of my thigh. Then, he moved his fingers in the opposite direction – up – until he cupped a cheek and looked me in the eye.

"You are so, so beautiful..."

All I could do was curve my lips up into a smile. The way he looked at me rendered me speechless. There were so many things I could and wanted to tell him – how hot he was, how I couldn't wait, how I couldn't believe he wanted to have sex with me – but in that moment, I just couldn't. His piercing blue eyes looked at me with so much intensity I was frozen, scared to make a move for fear that I'd do something wrong and he'd change his mind and walk away.

Before I could psyche myself out, Jake placed a tough hand on my waist and crashed his lips against mine impatiently. My eyes went wide at the realization of what was happening before I closed them and threw my cares to the air. Overthinking and worrying about what he was going to think or whether I was doing the right thing was futile. I just needed to let go of my inhibitions and trust that all the porn I'd watched wouldn't fail me.

I started to move my lips against his, starting with slow and smooth, until I felt him kiss harder. Then, his tongue swiped my bottom lip before I opened my mouth wider, my tongue meeting his. His hand moved up and down my side as the other held a tight grip around the back of his neck. After a while, he pulled away and began to plant a trail of soft kisses down my jaw and then my neck.

"Shit," I breathed as he bit down on the curve of my neck and began to lick and kiss. I hadn't ever felt this sensation before, and it was amazing. If being kissed on the neck already felt like this, I couldn't wait to experience what being fucked was like. "So, so…good."

"I knew you'd like that," he said, pulling away once more for a quick second, before he went back to exploring me. "I can't stop touching you...you're so, so..."

"I'm all yours," I said, finding the courage to say such words. I was getting hotter and wetter by the second and hoped my impatience wasn't showing. All I wanted was to see him naked and have him inside me. If he continued this kind of foreplay, I felt like I was going to explode and would have no energy when the time called for it. Just the way he kissed and touched me was making me feel hot and tired. I didn't want to disappoint him when the moment came.

He promised me the best 'first time'; I wanted to give him an equally great time tonight as well.

"Like this?" he asked with a smirk, grabbing one breast as his hand met the flimsy material of my sundress. "And this?" A single finger trailed up the lace of my panties, covering my pussy, and all I could do was nod my head in eagerness. "How about this?"

Before I knew it, he ripped my dress in half, unhooked my bra, and then closed his lips around my nipple as his two fingers began to rub up and down my panties. I arched my back off the bed, having never felt this before. I'd touched myself many times in the same areas, but having someone else touch me just felt so, so different and so much better.

I bit down – hard – on the skin of his shoulder when I felt his finger draw invisible circles on my clit. My breaths grew louder and raspier; my nails dug into his skin, and my pussy clenched tighter. As if that wasn't enough. With one hand, he pulled my panties off me before he stuck a finger inside me, and I pushed my back off the bed and into an arc when he made it two. I shut my eyes tight when he started to move his hand, fingers inside me, his thumb massaging my clit, and his mouth licking and biting my left breast. This overload of pleasure – it was the best thing ever, and it wasn't even sex yet. I'd begun to thrust my hips; I just couldn't get enough, and as I thrusted my entire lower torso higher so his hands could dig deeper inside me, I felt the build-up stirring.

This quick and this fast? I couldn't help but think as he continued to move his fingers in and out, motions growing quicker by the second. I knew I was about to come. I just couldn't believe he had the power to make me finish so quickly. There was no way I could do it this fast with myself.

"Fuck, Jake…I'm gonna come…I'm gonna come…"

"Come all over my hand…do it," he said, moving his mouth from my breast to my lips. I let out a strangled moan, his lips blocking mine, as I felt the dam break inside me and my liquid lathered his fingers. His hand continued to move, slower this time though, as my head fell back on the bed, and I tried to even my breathing.

"Jake…that was-" He planted a quick, hard kiss on my lips before he stretched his hand out towards his bedside table and opened the top drawer. My eyes widened when he took out a vibrator. "But I just-"

"So?" The smirk on his face was unmistakable. He placed the vibrator on the bed as he got up and began to strip. It only dawned on me that I'd been completely naked, and he still hadn't removed a single article of clothing. The idea just made me feel horny all over again. Him dressed while I was fully naked was just such a hot and sexy display of power. Now though, as I stared at the hard lines and muscles defining every inch of his skin, I was a witness to a different layer of sexiness and power. This was sexiness and power through hard work, and I just could not stop looking. Then, he reached for the vibrator and turned it on.

"You're not the only one who went shopping. Now you're going to come all over my dick."

JAKE.

I watched as her eyes widened, and I just couldn't help but edge the tip of my lips into a confident smirk. Then, I tipped my head downwards and admired the sight before me. My dick was flushed with her cum; it was hard and fully erect and was ready for her. I felt like I was in my own paradise at just thinking that I'd made her finish twice in minutes. I'd been with women who never came. I'd been with a rare few who finished just by me sticking a finger or dick in, without me even moving yet. Becca's body seemed like the perfect fit for mine, and I loved it.

"And now..." Her eyes grew bigger as I positioned the tip of my dick right at her entrance. Her legs had been splayed out widely for my fingers, mouth, and vibrator. She was ready; I could see the lips of her pussy, pulsating, squeezing, and then relaxing with the excitement of what was about to happen.

"B-but I just came!" she almost shouted, lifting her back off the bed to shorten the distance of our eye contact. "Jake, I don't even know if I-"

I kissed her hard to silence her, and she eagerly responded and pecked me back.

"Relax, I'm here...I didn't only promise to stretch out your first time for as long as I could, but I also told you I'd give you the best sex of your life."

"Exactly! How can we have the best sex if I feel so tired with barely having done anything." At those words, I saw her cheeks begin to flush pink. I found her response and reaction so cute, and my dick agreed with a single throb, flicking her clit just a bit.

"Becca, everything's going to be fine. Just relax, and don't think about it too much..." I reassured her. This time, I kissed her forehead. "Sex isn't like boarding school where we need to have plans and be prepared for everything...where wearing the wrong pair of socks can send us to the principal's office. Sex is about learning together. We can just...be."

At that, she grew silent and pursed her lips. She looked like she was thinking deeply about it until she finally turned to me and nodded her head. After a second or two, she exhaled deeply and watched me expectantly. As I pushed myself inside her, I leaned my head downwards to meet her lips. I knew this was going to hurt for her, and so, I kissed her to take her focus away from her hymen breaking. That, and her lips felt so soft; I could kiss her all day, every day. I suddenly grinned against the kiss as I remembered our agreement. She'd move in with me for an entire month and give me sex on-demand. I couldn't help the sudden animalistic instinct. It was everything about her – the way she looked, moved and talked, and *fuck...*

I closed my eyes as I felt the warmth of her insides. I then groaned when I felt her squeeze her inner walls.

"Relax...it'll be okay...we'll take it slowly," I said, continuing to kiss her.

When I couldn't go any further, I began to move my hips up and down. I started slow – as I'd told her I would – and opened my eyes to make sure she wasn't in any pain. She looked like she was taking me fine. I could sense a little bit of discomfort with how tightly she shut her eyes, but she wasn't telling me to stop. *Good.* When I felt her begin to rock her hips to meet mine, I then sped the thrusting just a little bit, and soon after, I was moving like my life depended on it, and I could feel my cum building up inside me.

Fuck yes.

I slowed down with the pumping until there was nothing else left before I pulled my dick out and watched as my creamy liquid dripped and flooded her pussy. I tipped my lips slightly downward at the sight of blood, and I didn't think twice about carrying her in my arms and walking to the bathroom. I set her down on the cool tiles before I turned the shower on and let the water wash away our sweat and her blood.

"That was…amazing…" she said as I soaped and massaged her pussy. I glanced at it a bit and noticed it was clean, no more sight of red. *Good.* "Thank you…"

"Who said I was done?" The smirk was back on my face again.

"You mean-"

"I'm just getting started." To get my point across, my fingers moved up from the lips of her pussy to her clit. As I moved my hand in a circular motion, I could feel her leaning her entire body onto mine as the sensation was becoming difficult for her to stand upright. That just did wonders for my ego. Everything about her was…I just had no words. "You're all mine now…for thirty days…I'm going to make the most out of it, and you…"

I was staring right at her.

"You've never been touched…you've never been

fucked." She wrapped her arm around the back of my shoulders while one hand moved to pleasure my growing erection. "And I'm the only one who gets to touch you and fuck you in ways that will make you scream."

7

ake

It'd been a week since we made the agreement — a week since she'd moved in with me. I knew I needed to get out if I wanted to save myself. I needed to get out of...*this*. I didn't want to admit it, but it was punching me right in the balls.

I was falling for her.

Everything about her just drew me in, and I almost laughed out loud at the idea. She was the embodiment of the society I hated and turned my back away from. She was daddy's little girl who got everything she needed and wanted. She never had to work a day in her life, didn't know what 'living paycheck to paycheck' meant; She was the type to spend thousands of dollars on a single shopping spree. She couldn't leave my loft without any make-up on. When I invited her to go out on a hike, she met me wearing a sundress and rubber slippers. She was so, *so* naïve. I should've been laughing at her. But I always found myself laughing *with* her.

She was naïve, but she was the most compassionate person I'd ever met. When I told her about how I pursued my passion instead of following my father's success plan as we laid in bed once night, she was all ears and asked question after question, showing genuine interest with my life – my life, which wasn't the type of life she deserved. I couldn't take her out to the best restaurants in town. I needed to pay the bills for my loft and tattoo parlor, and I also had staff to pay. Instead, she suggested cooking meals together. Her excuse was she wanted to learn before college began, but I really appreciated her for doing so. I'd dated girls who kept demanding, demanding, and then demanding some more. But Becca, who had the right to demand for the life she was given, never demanded for anything…except for sex. She demanded I take away her virginity, and I milked it for all I could.

I met her as a virgin, but in a span of a week, she'd learned and grown so much; we were both learning new things *together*. She told me the body parts where she loved being touched and pleasured; I told her how she could get better at hand jobs – a tighter grip. She was always willing to learn, inside and outside the bedroom, and just her curiosity for life, and mine specifically, was making me fall into an abyss I knew I couldn't get out of.

I wanted her to be completely mine; I didn't want anyone else to have her; I wanted her all to myself, so much so that I wanted to mark her...permanently. I wanted to draw a permanent masterpiece on her, one that told the world she was mine. It was such a dangerous thought, and I almost smirked outright at the irony. People always told me I was a dangerous man – they'd judged me just because of the ink on my body. I was learning now that virgin girls in pink dresses and satin sandals could be equally dangerous as well.

"You like that, huh?"

Her soothing, feminine voice instantly cut my train of thought, and I turned the machine off and put away the needle. I gave myself an internal reminder to get a new one later. If I left the needle out too long, it'd be bad to continue to use it.

"Hmmm?" I said, pushing myself off my chair and learning towards her for a quick peck.

. . .

I THEN LEANED BACKWARDS AND ADMIRED HER. SHE WAS getting just her hip bone tattooed but she was completely naked on the chair. I knew I was supposed to focus just on her hip, but I was so very tempted to ignore the bone and just go in for the pussy, not with the needle of course – my finger. Even better, my dick.

"When I play with your hair," she was quick to respond, and I forced myself to keep the throbbing feeling in my jeans at bay. The erection could wait for later. I needed to actually finish her tattoo. "You always look like a cat trying to nuzzle your head closer to me." Before I could say something, she added, "But I like it... no, I *love* it."

"It's comforting, yeah," I said, edging my lips into a smile. I was the guy women were warned about. Suffice to say, there wasn't a line of people wanting to play with my hair and cuddle with me. They always expected me to be rough and dirty. Sex with me wasn't about rainbows and butterflies; it was rough, hard, and the kind not everyone could handle. And the thought of Becca right now, stroking my hair, warmed me to my core. She could do all she wanted to me. "It also makes me sleepy, and you wouldn't want that right now."

I stretched the skin of her hip bone, admiring my art on her body. The butterfly design was halfway done, and when I looked at the clock and then saw the smirk on Becca's face, I knew why she had that look.

"Well, if you didn't keep stopping to kiss me...*everywhere*...we'd probably be done right now," she teased, eliciting an adorable laugh, and then, her tone sobered up slightly. "This is amazing...I love the textures of the lines...and it isn't even done yet...*wow*."

"Of course, it's done by me," I said, leaning forward again, this time to bite her ear.

"See, what did I just say? We're really never going to finish. We're going to be here all night, Jake," she responded, slapping my shoulder teasingly. My insides melted at that face of hers. Her smile was definitely her best feature although she wanted it to be her breasts.

"Are you complaining?" I couldn't help but add a raised eyebrow to that.

Before she responded, I already knew what her answer was going to be.

"Of course, not. Now, hurry up," she said, squeezing her legs together, and when I stared at her, it was her turn to give me a kiss. "I'm getting horny. Lying here naked definitely doesn't help."

Fuck. I pressed my growing erection against the chair, trying to control it, but it was futile. There was no way I could think with my head instead of my dick with a naked Becca right in front me.

For the tattoo. Finish it. I tried to kid myself. I shook my head, pushing all thoughts of sex to the back of my head temporarily. Then, I reached for a brand-new needle, stuck it into the tattoo gun, and put all my effort into focusing on getting the butterfly completed. I needed to do it justice, the art was a memory of her mother. 'My little butterfly' – that was her mother's nickname for her when she was still alive. I needed to do it justice; I needed to do my best – for the woman right in front of me.

I didn't know how long I took; I didn't care to look at the clock. All I knew was that after being stuck in the room for so long – admittedly, partly my fault for the temptress in front of me – I finally finished the butterfly, and I couldn't be any prouder. We spent the whole night yesterday coming up with different variations of Becca's inspiration image. I'd shown her almost ten hand drawn butterfly designs and kept refining them until there was one she not only liked but fell in love with. She was going to have it on her skin forever; she needed to love it. Now that it was done, she had the widest smile on her face, and it made me equally ecstatic to know I was the reason for her smiling.

"Thank you...so, *so* much," she said, almost losing her breath towards the end of her sentence. "Just wow...it's even much better on my skin than on paper."

"I'm glad you liked it," I said, putting my equipment away and giving her my full attention. There was no way I'd let her start dressing up when I had her naked on a chair for *hours. No way.* "And now…"

She turned her eyes away from her hip bone to find

me grinning mischievously at her. Before she knew it, I'd pulled her into my arms, her legs encircling my waist, and pushed her down on the table right beside the chair. Both of us becoming extremely impatient, our hands worked together to unbuckle and unzip my jeans. With one strong arm, she pushed my boxers all the way done, and I smirked when her eyes widened at the sight of my erection.

"Now," she said, propping her elbows on the table and spreading her legs out wide. I was a bit shocked when she wanted to get right to it, but my questions were answered as I began to glide my dick in smoothly inside her. She was *so fucking* wet. There was no need to finger or tease her or start with foreplay. We'd have time for sweet and romantic in bed later. Right now, we were going to have it quick, easy, and rough – a different side to the both of us.

"F-fuck…y-you," she tried breathing, as I pumped in and out in front of her. I felt like the table was going to give out anytime soon, but to hell with that, just her wetness was ready to make finish now. "Sex with you just keeps getting better and better."

"It takes two," I said, as I crashed my lips against hers and added some teeth. She moaned at the roughness and held onto me tighter.

"R-Jake…I'm gonna com-I'm gonna come…"

"Me too," I said, biting on her bottom lip. "Together."

And with that, I pounded into her much faster now, and she clung to me as if her life depended on it.

We were only week in. I never wanted the next three weeks to come. I wanted her, all to myself, forever.

8

ecca

THIS DIDN'T NEED TO HAPPEN. IT WAS THE housekeeper's fault – a hundred per cent. If she wasn't such a tattletale and told my father I had rarely been home in the past twenty-eight days, we wouldn't be in this situation. She was always looking for ways to get me in trouble, and I knew why. She had to slave all day and work for a spoiled, entitled princess – me.

I'd already told my dad I was sleeping over at Mary's and Jane's, but *she* just had to whip up this story of how I kept disappearing from time to time, and how on the first day I left, I brought with me a huge luggage full of clothes. Just thinking about what was happening made my blood boil. She never did this when my half-sisters were around. They were much older than I was, and so, there was no way she could tell lies to my dad, and have my father pick the help over his own daughters, my half-sisters. My dad loved them; they followed the path he carved out for them unquestioned, and they were on top of the world, heading and managing many of my dad's ventures. I loved them too; they were always looking out for me, stood as the mother figures in my life since my mom died.

But they weren't here right now – when I needed them. But I doubt they'd understand. The idea of a man keeping me for thirty days to have sex whenever and wherever he desired wouldn't ease anyone's nerves, and now my father was demanding to know where I'd been the past weeks.

I finally broke, scared of what could happen if I disobeyed my father, and told him a half-lie, half-truth. I told him I was staying with my boyfriend, and now, Jake and I were on the way to meet my father for lunch.

"It's going to be okay, I'm here," he said, trying to reassure me. He reached out to rest a hand on my shoulder, squeezed, and pulled back his arm.

The gesture calmed me down a little, but my inner self was telling me it was a futile move. We were twenty-eight days into our agreement; two more days then I'd have to walk out. At that thought, I immediately felt a stabbing pain in my chest. There was no denying it. By spending every waking and sleeping moment with him for the past weeks, there was no way I wouldn't fall for him.

But I was just a diversion.

He'd popped the virgin's cherry. He was done with what he wanted to do, succeeded in making his fetish a reality, and after a couple of days, he'd be back on the market, dating and fucking supermodels and more mature women who looked like goddesses and had the sexual experience I could only dream of.

"What are you thinking about?" Jake then asked, breaking my train of thought. I watched as he pulled my car up into the driveway of the five-star hotel. Our doors were opened by the valet attendants waiting, and Jake handed one the keys before we stepped into the hotel.

I felt Jake take my hand as we were greeted by a grand double staircase and gold-rimmed and marble columns. When I turned to look at him, there was a hint of unease with the way his lips were tight and shut. He didn't feel like he fit in; I knew what he felt, but I'd told him repeatedly he didn't need to care. He walked away from *this* life; it didn't deem him unsuitable. No one could, not even his self-entitled, snobby family.

Or so I thought.

"Fuck," I heard him breathe as we walked into the

restaurant at the topmost floor where my father booked us a reservation.

I turned my head and followed his line of vision and let out a string of my own expletives. I should have expected this. *Why didn't I see this coming?* Of course, my father and Jake's would have lunch together regularly. They were doing business together.

"So, this is your new boyfriend?" The look on both businessmen's faces were unmistakable.

"What are you talking about, Connor?" The elder Huntington said, sitting up straighter on his seat and tapping his ring on the table. The knocking sound it made was slightly annoying.

"My daughter has been gone for almost a month, not sleeping or eating or showering in the house. She said she had a boyfriend. Apparently, it's your son."

Before I could speak my mind, my dad started off. He began raising his voice, not caring if a few heads were starting to turn to look at us. My dad expected everyone to bow down to him, even strangers. This situation was no exception; he didn't care if he was causing a scene because he expected the world to accept what he wanted, no questions asked.

"Haven't I warned you enough times about Harry's delinquent son?" I stiffened when he said 'delinquent'. Now my father was just exaggerating. Jake was anything but. He was passionate, hardworking, and empathetic. "Didn't I tell you he was an ungrateful brat who ran away from the family who'd given him everything? Why don't you ever listen to me, Becca? Why can't you see I just want what's best for you? Why are you always looking for trouble?"

"By the best you mean, the richest, most successful man you can hook me up with?" I said, trying to control my anger. There was no changing my dad's mind. We'd had this kind of argument countless times before. He'd always try to drag me to his high-society events and force me to talk to his friends' children in the hopes I'd get into a relationship with any one of them and secure a future of success and wealth most of the world's population could only dream of. "I don't need that. Jake is-"

"Sorry, dear," my father cut me off. "The world runs on currency. You just have to accept it."

"Do you just have to go around and ruin someone else's life? Aren't you satisfied with ruining your own future?" That was Harry Huntington speaking, his voice booming and authoritative, and the lawyer in him surfacing. I turned my head to the side to gauge Jake's reaction, and I couldn't be any prouder. He stood tall, unwavering, and held his own ground despite the toxic words coming out of his father's mouth. No wonder our fathers were such good colleagues and friends. They were just two peas in a pod. "Don't ruin her future like you ruined your own. You don't deserve her. What can you give to her that her father hasn't already have? Last time I heard, your tattoo place is barely surviving. Do you know that?" He then turned to address me. "He only has enough money to keep himself afloat."

That was it. I couldn't handle the shit they were throwing at him anymore. My father spouting out words of discouragement by himself was bad enough but having him and Jake's dad doing it together? Any person could only take so much before they'd crumble.

"Shut up." I winced at my own words; I knew I was digging my own grave, but I was too infuriated to care. "You don't know anything about him. You've been out of his life for years. You haven't seen how he's touched people's lives, how he uses his art to connect with the world around him because all you two care about is the bottom line." My hands were balled into fists at my sides; I felt like I had so much emotions running through me, so many feelings I wanted to let out. "He started his own business to follow his own passion, not to rob the world, so you two can just become richer and richer. I've never met more selfish people than you two."

"Y-you-"

"I'm not finished," I said, glaring at my dad. I didn't know where this newfound courage came from, but it was allowing me to let out feelings I'd bottled up inside for years. "Don't tell me who to date and cannot date. Too late. I love Jake...he's been there for me when you were absent…he's been there to listen to me and take care of me. I love him…as much as I do mom," I carried on, my fingers on the waistband of my shorts. "I got a tattoo…" I pulled the denim slightly down to give them a view of the butterfly. "It's what mom used to call me. There's not better art than bringing the two people I care most about in this world together. Thank you for nothing, dad. You've been telling me you just want what's best for me, but I know the truth; you want to carve my life just so you can pad your own pocket." Then, my eyes swerved to meet Jake's father's. "The both of you can go to hell."

And with that, I grabbed Jake's hand and led the way out of the restaurant. There was no turning back.

9

ake

SHE LOVES ME.

She really loves me.

All throughout my life, I was told that showing emotions was a sign of weakness. I built a wall so high that nothing scared me. People could threaten me, and I wouldn't give a damn. When my father told me that he'd leave me out of the will if I didn't go to law school, I gathered the strength to turn my back on him and walk away. When I experienced my first heartbreak in high school, it only made me stronger and mysterious that I learned to play the cool, unaffected façade so well it attracted so many girls and women. When I'd gotten into some fistfights, I can come out would bruises and wounds but never a bruised ego. I could handle a lot, almost nothing perturbed me.

Except for her.

With her holding my hand tightly, I could feel myself shaking a bit. I was so overwhelmed with so much emotions that I just wanted to take her in my arms, kiss the living daylights out of her, and do things to her that would get us kicked out of and banned from the hotel.

She loves me.

The thought kept replaying in my head. She stood up to both our dads and basically told them to fuck off. No one would ever dare do that to them. I'd done it to my father once, but he already expected that kind of attitude from me. But Becca...sweet, innocent, and compassionate Becca...all along I thought that she needed me to be the stronger one, the one to protect her from the harshness of life. I was so, *so* naïve.

She didn't need any protecting. She was stronger than I gave her credit for, and the strength she'd been hiding came out today. I was the one that needed protecting today.

She rocked me to my core. No one had ever told those two men to fuck off, not even their wives could say such a profanity outright. Becca had no idea how impressed I was...how much I appreciated just what she did. And I wanted to let her know. I wanted to show her just how much I loved her and appreciated her for standing up for me. Usually, I showed it by ravishing her until she came while screaming my name. With her, pleasuring her never felt like a chore. I could tease and lick her full breasts all day and finger and eat her out until she finished and grew sore. I loved making her happy. I loved pleasuring and servicing her. I'd never felt this before. It was everything about her that was making me feel so overwhelmed right now.

I wanted to show her how much I loved her and cared. But of course, I just couldn't fuck her in such a public place.

She loves me. And I love her too. But how will I show it?

Then, it came to me. It was so automatic and felt so natural that I didn't even think about it. I just found myself dropping to one knee and meeting her hazel eyes. She looked shocked, her mouth opening into a small 'o' and her arm stiffening as she looked down on me on one knee. For a quick second, I glanced to the side and saw both our fathers watching us. The whole floor of the hotel had their eyes on us. They heard the argument between us and our fathers. Now, everyone wanted in on the aftermath.

"I've known you for over eight years, but I'd only really gotten to know you for close to one month…" Becca looked like she was about to cry, but the smile on her face gave me the strength to continue. "But in that month, I found out how much of an amazing person you were...you *are*. You could've judged me straight away. If you told anyone about our month-long agreement, everyone would've warned you to stay away from me." I took a pause and continued. This feeling inside me – the fucking butterflies and knots in my stomach – I was feeling more overwhelmed than what I felt just a few minutes ago. "But you stayed, and for the first time in a very, *very* long time, I felt like someone actually really cared about me. You make me feel love and cared for, and that's irreplaceable with the life I'm trying to live – trying to succeed on my own when my own family doesn't believe in me." I swallowed my own breath, pushing the fear away, and parted my lips to ask, "I need someone to hold my hand, to be my strength when I am weak, and that someone's you. I've never been surer of anything..." And then, finally, "Becca Madison, will you marry me?"

Tears spilled out of her eyes as she cupped my cheeks in her soft, feminine hands. She pulled me to stand up, and she pressed her lips softly against mine. I couldn't help but smile instantly when I felt the emotions in her kiss and the tears on her flesh. After what felt like forever, I pulled away. If we didn't stop kissing, things would've have become more intense and required parental guidance.

"Of course..." she began, still sobbing. "Of course, I'll marry you."

Then, I followed the movement of her eyes. She moved her head down and looked at her hands, and instantly, I knew what to say. "The ring...I want it be another tattoo. I can draw little butterflies and our initials around your finger...I want it in ink instead of metal because that way, you can never remove it. I plan on having you all to myself for a very, *very* long time..."

She parted her lips, smile growing wider, as she reached for my hand. All around, people were snapping photographs and taking videos of us. Some were still applauding and cooing at my proposal. I could also feel our fathers trying to burn a hole through the back of our heads, but with so much love and support surrounding us, I couldn't give a damn.

"Then let's go home...I want the *both of us* to design the ring."

And I'd never heard a plan more perfect.

EPILOGUE

I'd always loved the 'Winter Wonderland' theme ever since I started going to school parties and dances, and it was only now that I truly understood why. I looked around the church, and from behind the windows, I could see snow falling, cooling the church and making me feel relaxed and completely at peace.

I was attending my own wedding, but I was thinking of so many things that I wasn't listening to the priest anymore.

I knew I should listen to the ceremony. I didn't become a bridezilla for the past six months for nothing. But the truth was, there were so many wonderful things I could set my sights on right here, right now. The entire church was adorned in Christmas lights in a white-and-blue color palette. Humongous ornaments of ribbons and snow balls adorned the marble walls and columns. Warm yellow lighting illuminated the entire vicinity to give off a very intimate ambiance. The choir we'd hired sang with such expertise that just listening could ignite a variety of emotions from within.

Most importantly was the man right beside me, and our family and friends watching and supporting us in this momentous occasion.

The past six months had been a roller coaster of ups and downs. It took a while for our families to finally accept we were getting married. Over the course of those months, they gradually started to see that our love for one another was unbreakable and authentic. With my social network in the city, I helped Jake drive his business forward, and from his business' earnings, he supported me as I started college. I'd been living with him, and he'd been covering our living expenses. I'd also taken a part-time job as a receptionist in the local hospital. I wanted to prove to myself and to my family that I could succeed with the path I carved out on my own. Looking back at what I'd experienced the past months, I would do everything all over again. My father admired my strength; my half-sisters told me

His Dirty Virgin

they felt a little jealous of how I was able to stand up to our dad.

And today, here at Jake's and my wedding, we had our friends and family bearing witness to our love and commitment to one another.

"You're the best gift I've been given…more than what I could ever hope for and deserve…I love you so, so much, Becca Huntington. I can't wait to call you my wife."

"I love you, Jake…more than life itself…you have no idea. I can't wait to spend the rest of my life with you."

With a single nod, the priest smiled at the simplicity of our words and finally said, "Becca and Jake, you have expressed your love and commitment to one another with the vows you've just made. You're no longer simply girlfriend and boyfriend, no longer just partners and best friends. Now, you have become husband and wife." And with a larger smile, he continued, "Jake, you may now kiss your bride."

Looking back at the past six months in my head, I smiled at thought of looking forward to forever with the man right in front of me, my husband.

The End.

ABOUT THE AUTHOR

Jessa James grew up on the East Coast but always suffered a severe case of wanderlust. She's lived in six states, had a variety of jobs and always comes back to her first true love – writing. Jessa works full time as a writer, eats too much dark chocolate, has an iced-coffee and Cheetos addiction, and can't get enough of sexy alpha males who know exactly what they want – and aren't afraid to say it. Dominant, alpha-male insta-luv is her favorite to read (and write).

Sign up HERE for Jessa's VIP Reader List
http://bit.ly/JessaJames

Find Jessa Online
jessajamesauthor.com

WANT MORE? READ LIP SERVICE

Carter: She's mine. I want her. I need her and I'm tired of waiting.

Emma: He's all I think about but I can't wait for him any longer. Tonight's the night. I'm punching my V-card.

LIP SERVICE - CHAPTER 1

Carter Buchanan, Billionaire, President of Buchanan Industries — Biotech Division

EMMA WALKED OUT OF THE CONFERENCE ROOM, HER luscious ass swinging side to side in that fucking pencil skirt and I couldn't tear my gaze from her curves. Not even when my cock grew hard as granite beneath the table. I had it bad for Emma. Bad. I sported the worst case of blue balls imaginable and it was all because of her.

She'd waltzed into my office a year ago with an armful of files, introduced herself as my brother, Ford's, new secretary, and I'd almost come in my pants then and there. My brother had all the fucking luck.

Since that first moment, when I saw her perfect tits framed in that tight, black sweater, her wide hips and perfect ass hugged by long linen pants, I could think of nothing but bending her over my desk and making her mine.

But the company had a strict hands-off policy. Hell, so did I. But HR would have a lawsuit on their hands if they knew all of the ways I wanted to fuck her, to claim those curves, even if she worked for Ford in a completely different department.

It wasn't just her body that drove me insane—and made my dick constantly hard—it was her sharp mind, too. Overqualified for her job, she made Ford's work life easy. She'd swooped in and organized our joint production schedules the first week, making the previous assistant seem a bumbling fool and giving my secretary, Tori, some much needed relief. Emma knew what Ford and I needed even before we did. Hell, the other execs, too. I considered putting her up for a promotion, but then I'd miss hearing her softly pitched, "Good morning, Carter," as she waltzed into the staff meeting every Tuesday and Thursday morning at precisely 8:00 am.

Yes, all those fucking thoughts—and thoughts about fucking—made me an asshole, but I hadn't touched her. I'd imagined it so many different ways, but all of them had one thing in common. I'd fuck her raw, no condom, and I'd fill her with my cum. I'd shoot it so far inside her, and so often, that she'd never be able to wash the scent of me from her body. She'd be marked as mine. Yes, every fuck fest in my head ended with me claiming her in the most elemental of ways, filling her with my baby as I made her writhe and beg for release.

Not very gentlemanly of me. But every time I saw her, my Ivy League education and analytical mind devolved about a million years. I changed into something primal. A caveman. I wanted to tangle my fingers in her hair and drag her into my office and fuck her. Make sure she knew exactly who she belonged to.

I'd discreetly asked my brother about her on several occasions. Ford had told me to fuck off and find my own secretary. And that was why I'd left her alone for the last twelve months. I wasn't just an asshole, I was an *old* asshole. Ten years her senior. I was ready to settle down, to get on with that house with the picket fence, the two kids and a fucking Labrador Retriever. She made me think crazy thoughts, want things I never imagined I'd want. But I did. I wanted that fucking house. I wanted her round and pregnant with my baby. I even wanted the fucking dog. But only with her.

Unfortunately, she wasn't ready. Emma was just twenty-four and needed to live a little before a dominating caveman like me took over her life. Once she was mine, I'd want total control. I'd fuck her when

I wanted to, pamper her the way I wanted to, make sure she came so many times on my hard cock that she never looked at another man again. I'd ruin her, and she wasn't ready for that. Not for what I wanted to give her. I'd waited a year already and she graduated in a few weeks with a Master's in Finance. Yeah, she could analyze my fucking numbers anytime.

Sure, I'd waited like a fucking gentleman, tried to give her the space she needed to sow her wild oats. I figured I could wait a few more weeks.

At least, that was the plan. But when I heard her voice drifting down the hallway from the copy room, everything changed.

"I hate being a virgin," she said. I doubted she knew her voice carried, but I was glad it was me that heard her confession. If it had been anyone else who knew her secret, I'd have to beat the shit out of them. No one messed with Emma. She might be Ford's secretary, but she was mine.

I was walking past, heading back to the elevators after our Thursday meeting on the fourteenth floor when I recognized her voice. It was her words though, that had me leaning against the wall and out of sight. Eavesdropping. She'd turned me into a fucking eavesdropper. No, the fact that she'd said she was a virgin had.

"There's nothing wrong with being a virgin." I

recognized the voice of my secretary, Tori. She was in her late twenties, single, and gorgeous. I told her that she should go out with Ford, but she just raised a brow and told me she'd sworn off men. She'd worked for me just over a year but I didn't know more than that. And with the *don't-fuck-with-me* look in her eyes, I didn't ask for details. I didn't have time to dig into her personal life. As usual, she was efficient and professional, and I thought her words to Emma were sound.

"I'm twenty-four, Tori. I must be the oldest virgin on earth."

I thought of her, untouched, pure. God, just knowing that pussy hadn't been fucked had me shifting my cock. I had to look down the hall to ensure no one could see me with my dick hard.

"So a few more days, weeks, hell, months, isn't going to make a difference. Trust me on that one." The woman deserved a promotion for that answer.

"That guy Jim ran out of my apartment when I told him I'd never had sex before. He called me a unicorn. What the hell does that even mean?"

I heard the copier door open, then close. The machine kicked on.

"He was an asshole," Tori replied.

Thank fuck he was an asshole. I didn't even know who the hell Jim was, but he didn't deserve my sweet Emma, or her virgin pussy.

"I'm telling you, don't do it. Some guy at a bar is not who you want to give your V card to," Tori said.

What guy at what bar? I stood up straight and leaned closer.

"Well, that V card is in my way. No guy wants to deal with a virgin, Tori. I'm like a kid playing in the grown-up pool. It's just one night and then it's over. I can put the stupid virginity thing behind me and move on."

No one wanted to deal with her? Hell, she was perfect as she was. Girl next door perfect and I'd been afraid I'd corrupt her. I wasn't a good guy. Hell, I'd worked my way through enough women to know what they thought of me. I was—used to be—the fuck-em and leave-em type, but I'd never offered any of them more than one night and they all knew that going in. I'd only wanted a release, a short respite where I forgot everything in their willing bodies. I hadn't promised more. Ever. Had never wanted more. Until Emma. And I wanted to give her everything.

"Then pick someone to make it worth your while. We both know who you really want."

I heard Emma laugh, but the sound wasn't sweet, it was sad. "Yeah, that's so not going to happen. He doesn't even know I'm alive."

Tori laughed. "Maybe you should parade around naked. He'll notice, trust me. And I've heard he's fucking fantastic in bed."

"God, don't tell me things like that," Emma pleaded. "I already can't think when I'm around him."

"Seriously, woman. Why don't you dress up a little? Show some cleavage. You know, seduce him?"

"Right. Me? You've got to be kidding. I'm about as sexy as a kindergarten teacher." Emma sighed and I imagined her crossing her arms, knew the exact face she was probably making. "Hence the problem, Tori. Big, stupid virgin, remember? He wouldn't waste his time with me. He doesn't seem like the virgin type. Which is one of the reasons I want to get laid tonight."

Tonight? And who was my Emma pining for? Who the fuck was she talking about? Was Emma interested in someone? I'd never heard of her going on a date, and Ford kept pretty close tabs on everyone working for him. The office was small enough for me to find out what she was doing most of the time. Only Brad from Accounting had come sniffing around her last Thanksgiving and I'd shut him down easily enough. Who the hell was she longing for and why didn't I know about him? I was a jealous prick for wondering, but hell, I was selfish. I wanted her all to myself.

"I still think a one night stand with some guy you hook up with in a bar is a bad idea."

Bless Tori and her sage advice. Trouble was, my Emma wasn't listening.

"Look, Tori, it's fine. A stranger is better. If I'm terrible in bed, I'll never have to see him again. And I want to know what it's like to have a man inside me. I want him sweaty and bossy and so fucking hard he can't wait to fuck me. I want a real man. I want skin and kissing and a real cock, not battery-operated Bob."

My balls drew up at her words. She wanted skin? Kissing? A bossy man with a big cock?

I had a cock she could ride all damn night.

Tori laughed. "Fine, fine. You're a big girl. We'll meet tonight at Frankie's. Seven o'clock. If you're going to have a one-night-stand, I'll at least make sure you have condoms and the guy's not a serial killer."

"Thanks, Tori!" Emma was really excited. I knew that tone and it was the same one she'd used when flowers arrived at her desk on Valentine's Day. Two dozen long stem red roses from a secret admirer. Me.

Ford had called me himself and warned me to back off. Well, I had. Promising to wait until she graduated to make my move. But her plans for tonight changed everything.

The only cock Emma was going to have inside her tonight, or any fucking night, was mine.

When two men from finance headed my way, I turned and walked back the way I had come, ducking into the men's room. I didn't want Emma to know I'd been listening and I needed a few minutes to will my cock back into submission.

Fifteen minutes later, I sat behind my desk and

watched the sexiest fucking woman on the planet enter my office with the typed up reports from our morning meeting. Yeah, I could get the fucking things on email, but I liked them printed out and delivered. I was old fucking fashioned in that way, and wasn't about to change, especially if it brought her through my office door.

Emma set the report on the corner of my desk and didn't even look at me, which was probably a good thing, considering the way I devoured her curves with my eyes.

"It's five, Mr. Buchanan. Unless there's something else you need from our office, I'm going to call it a day."

I swallowed hard. Need? Yeah, there was something else I needed, but I wasn't going to take it here, in my office, with her skirt flipped up over her luscious ass and her head down on my desk.

At least, not yet. That would come later. When she knew who she belonged to. When her body knew it was mine.

"That's fine, Emma. Are you hitting the town with the rest of the staff for their usual Thursday night at Frankie's Bar?" The place was upscale, expensive, and offered exotic drinks like chocolate martinis. And it was only two blocks from the office. So, yeah, the bar had been a haunt of the Buchanan staff for years.

Her cheeks turned pink and she bit her lip, but she

also raised her head in surprise and met my gaze. I felt that bright, innocent stare down to my toes.

I imagined those big, round eyes sizing some stranger up at a bar. Accepting his offer to buy her a drink. Agreeing to go home with him. Taking off that tight fucking skirt and wrapping her legs around his waist.

Fuck.

I had to turn away, afraid she'd see the rage building in my head, buzzing like a hornets' nest. No one was fucking touching her. No one but me.

After counting to ten, I looked back up.

She grinned, picking at the corner of the notepad and papers she held in front of her chest. "Yes. Everyone's meeting there after work. How did you know about Frankie's? I've never seen you there before."

Standing slowly, I walked around the edge of my desk and stopped inches from her. More than anything, I wanted to pull her into my arms and forbid her from entering that meat market. I knew all too well just how many young, arrogant pricks would be there waiting to get their hands on a soft, curvy virgin like my Emma. They'd be dressed in their suits, hair slicked back, throwing hundred dollar bills on the bar to try to impress the ladies, trying to impress Emma.

Eyes growing wider, she watched me approach, but held her ground. That was my girl. I loved that spunk, that fucking fire. She'd never backed down, not once in all the months she'd worked for the Buchanans.

Unable to resist touching her, I lifted my hand to her shoulder in what I hoped wouldn't come off as an asshole move. She glanced down at my hand, confused, I was sure, because I'd never touched her before, but she didn't shrug me off.

I waited patiently for her to raise her gaze to mine. "I've never been invited."

"What?" Shock clouded her eyes, but she quickly blinked it away. "How? I mean, I'm sorry. I didn't know. I don't…that's not…I—"

She was so damn beautiful when she stuttered, and her obvious concern for my emotional well-being was adorable.

Leaning forward, I placed a chaste kiss on her cheek before stepping away. "Don't worry about me, Emma."

She gasped at the surprise contact, then bit her lip and stifled the sound. Her cheek was warm and silky soft beneath my lips. I wanted more, to find out if she was so damn soft everywhere else. And her scent…

"No," she replied. "I think you should come. Get to know everyone better. Maybe they wouldn't be so sc—"

Emma stopped herself just in time and I threw back my head with laughter. "Scared?"

Her blush was a deep, dark pink and I longed to trace the color all the way down her neck and under that blouse, discover if her breasts were as flushed as her face.

"I'm sorry." She sighed. "Look, I'm not usually such a mess. I don't normally—"

"Tell me the truth?" I cut her off.

She raised a brow, but met my gaze squarely. "I tell you the truth, but I don't tell tales."

"That's because you're smart."

It was her turn to laugh. "Apparently, not around you." Her gaze drifted lower, to my mouth, my lips, just for a moment, but I saw it, and I knew I would have her. Soon.

I squeezed her shoulder and reluctantly, let her go. "Go on, Emma. It's been a helluva week. You better go before they think I trapped you here for the weekend."

Trapped, under me. On top of me. Bent over my desk.

It was like my cock had taken over my head.

"See you next week." Emma walked out of my office without looking back, her soft blond hair swinging over her shoulders, her curvy ass sashaying as she left me standing there alone, like a dick.

I nearly ran after her. Instead, I fisted my hands in my pockets and told my cock to fucking stand down. Nothing was happening until later.

Nothing but me convincing Emma that I was the right man for her, the *only* man for her.

There was no fucking way Emma was giving her

virginity to some random fucker at a bar. She wanted cock? I had one she could take full advantage of. But it wasn't just one night I wanted. I wanted all her nights. I'd stayed away because she was pure, because I didn't want to risk ruining her with my base needs. And because I knew she had plans, was just finishing her degree. I was trying to be a god-damned gentleman and wait until she was ready.

That was over. If she was ready to give her body away, she damn well was going to give it to me and no one else. I wanted Emma. Her body was mine. Her smile was mine. That luscious mouth was mine to fuck. Her virginity, mine to take. I wouldn't share her. I couldn't stand by and watch her give herself to some random stranger all too eager to fuck her and forget her.

She deserved better than that and I was going to make sure she got it.

Forever. Yes, Emma was going to be mine tonight. After that, she wouldn't have any doubts about who she belonged to.

But first, I had to convince her that I wasn't playing around. I'd take her out to dinner and hold doors, that's what I'd do. I'd seduce her, make her scream with every orgasm, fill her wet pussy with my big, hard cock. I'd send her roses every fucking day and kiss her until she couldn't breathe. Eventually, I'd put my ring on her finger and my baby in her womb.

I'd claim her every way a man could claim his woman.

I was done trying to be noble, trying to protect her from my darkness. If she was ready for more, I was going to give it to her. Me. No one else.

She was mine, she just didn't know it yet.

Get Lip Service now!

GET A FREE BOOK!

Join my mailing list to be the first to know of new releases, free books, special prices and other author giveaways.

http://freehotcontemporary.com

ALSO BY JESSA JAMES

Bad Boy Billionaires

Lip Service

Rock Me

Lumber Jacked

Baby Daddy

The Virgin Pact

The Teacher and the Virgin

His Virgin Nanny

His Dirty Virgin

Club V

Unravel

Undone

Uncover

Bad Boys with Big Sticks Series

Fake Fiancé

Additional Titles

Beg Me

Valentine Ever After

ABOUT THE AUTHOR

Jessa James grew up on the East Coast but always suffered a severe case of wanderlust. She's lived in six states, had a variety of jobs and always comes back to her first true love – writing. Jessa works full time as a writer, eats too much dark chocolate, has an iced-coffee and Cheetos addiction, and can't get enough of sexy alpha males who know exactly what they want – and aren't afraid to say it. Dominant, alpha-male insta-luv is her favorite to read (and write).

Sign up HERE for Jessa's Newsletter:

http://jessajamesauthor.com/mailing-list/

www.ingramcontent.com/pod-product-compliance
Lightning Source LLC
LaVergne TN
LVHW011846060526
838200LV00054B/4196